Food +
Farming

To Bea –
L.S.

First published in the United Kingdom in 2002
by David Bennett Books Limited, an imprint of Chrysalis Books plc,
64 Brewery Road, London N7 9NT

Text and illustrations copyright © 2002 Lucy Su.
Lucy Su asserts her moral right to be identified
as the author and illustrator of this work.

BRITISH LIBRARY
CATALOGUING-IN-PUBLICATION DATA
A catalogue record for this book is available
from the British Library.

ISBN 1 85602 445 8
Printed in Singapore.

Kitten and Baby Kitten
Make a Picnic

Lucy Su

DAVID BENNETT BOOKS

Kitten and Baby Kitten were
quietly building a tower.
"Miaow!" cried Baby Kitten.
"I'm hungry."

Kitten looked at the clock.
It was time for lunch.
Outside the sun was shining.
"Let's have a picnic," said Kitten.
"Yes, yes, yes!" shouted Baby Kitten.

Kitten found some sardines, cheese, egg, jam, honey, lettuce and tomato.

"Yuck! Don't like egg,"
thought Baby Kitten.

Kitten liked to cut the sandwiches into different shapes. Baby Kitten always liked to watch and he liked to taste, too!

"Shall we have orange juice
or apple juice?" asked Kitten.
"Both!" shouted Baby Kitten.
He loved apple juice with
just a little bit of orange.

Kitten fetched some bananas, pears, grapes, oranges, cherries and apples.

Baby Kitten lined them up in rows!

Kitten and Baby Kitten
now had lots of bags and
boxes of food. Kitten placed
them one on top of another.
"Too many!" cried Baby Kitten.

Kitten found a basket,
but it was too small.

Then she found a trolley
in the cupboard.
"That's better," she said.

It was so warm outside
in the sunshine.

Kitten and Baby Kitten were
looking forward to their picnic.

Kitten laid out
the picnic.
Baby Kitten was
chasing a butterfly.
Kitten felt a plop of rain
but Baby Kitten didn't care.

"Come on, hurry!" called Kitten.

Baby Kitten was all wet
when he came inside but
he still wanted his picnic.

Kitten knew just what to do.

What a lovely picnic!

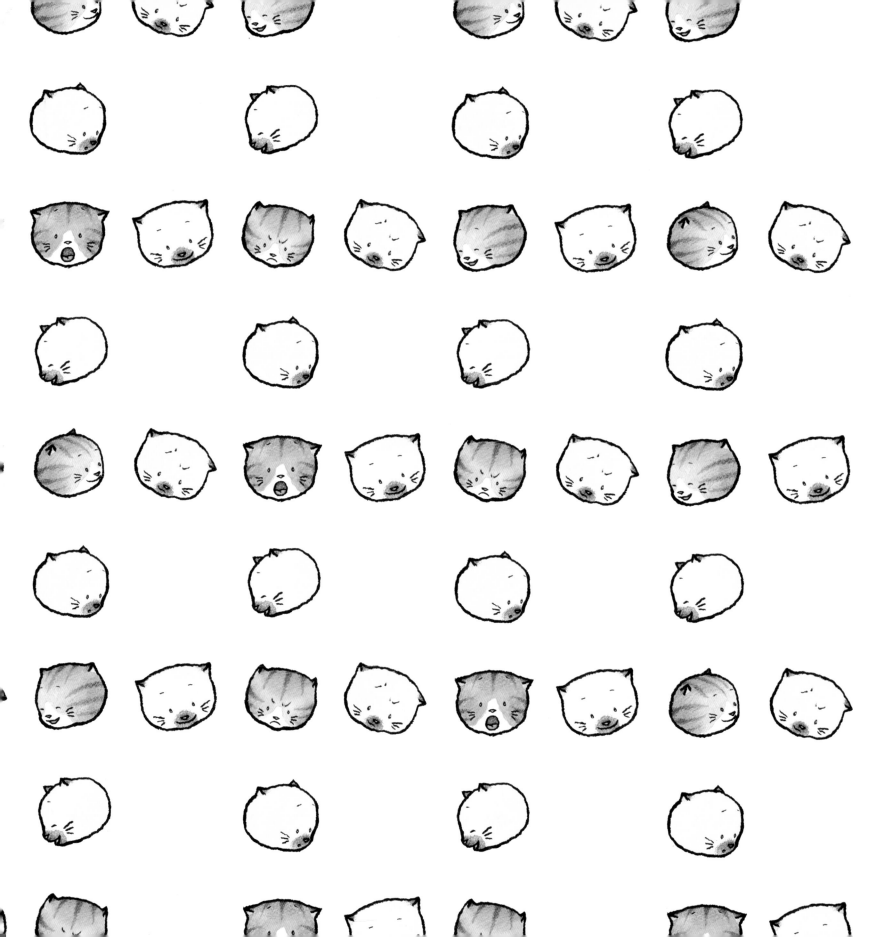